GHOSTBUSTER'S HANDBOOK

By Daphne Pendergrass

Simon Spotlight
New York   London   Toronto   Sydney   New Delhi

SIMON SPOTLIGHT
An imprint of Simon & Schuster Children's Publishing Division
1230 Avenue of the Americas, New York, New York 10020
This Simon Spotlight paperback edition June 2016
Ghostbusters TM & © 2016 Columbia Pictures Industries, Inc. All Rights Reserved.
All rights reserved, including the right of reproduction in whole or in part in any form.
SIMON SPOTLIGHT and colophon are registered trademarks of Simon & Schuster, Inc.
For information about special discounts for bulk purchases, please contact
Simon & Schuster Special Sales at 1-866-506-1949 or
business@simonandschuster.com.
Designed by Julie Robine
Manufactured in the United States of America 0516 LAK
ISBN 978-1-4814-7486-3
ISBN 978-1-4814-7487-0 (eBook)

Contents

CONFIDENTI

How to Use This Guide

So, you think you have what it takes to be a Ghostbuster?

You think grabbing ghouls, apprehending apparitions, or vanquishing vapors is the career for you?

Lesson One: Being a Ghostbuster is a serious science that requires serious training. If you run into a Class V ectoplasmic manifestation without the proper training, you could quickly find yourself waist-deep in a T3 interaction.

That's Ghostbuster-speak for pooping your pants.

Contained within these pages are some of our best-kept secrets for combatting ghostly threats. This book will act as a reference point for all your ghostbusting work from here on out. Guard it carefully. In the wrong hands a book can become a terrible weapon.

Important Ghostbusters and Their Contributions

ZHU'S AUTHENTIC HONG KONG FOOD

承接金豬
明爐烤鴨　蜜汁叉燒

Founding Member: Erin Gilbert, PhD

Dr. Erin Gilbert specializes in theoretical particle physics and has been published in journals such as *Nature* and *Scientific American*. Passionate yet practical, Erin is driven to see the Ghostbusters' paranormal research accepted by the scientific community at large.

Prior to founding Ghostbusters, Erin was up for tenure in the physics department at Columbia University. If Erin could pass her tenure review, she would become a permanent professor there. During her review the faculty discovered her ghost research at the Aldridge Mansion with fellow founding members Abby and Holtzmann. The university wanted nothing to do with what they deemed the pseudoscience of ghost hunting, and so Erin was fired soon after.

Columbia's loss became the Ghostbusters' gain, as Erin became instrumental in the battle to save New York City from Rowan the Destroyer, a Class VII metaspecter (see page 74).

– Ghost Girl –

Erin's interest in ghosts began at an early age. As a child Erin suffered a terrifying encounter with a Class IV entity:

When I was eight the mean old lady who lived next door to us died. That night I woke up and there she was, standing at the foot of my bed. She was just staring at me, and then blood started coming out of her mouth. She started slowly falling toward me. I pulled my covers over my head and waited until morning. She did that every night for a year.

Unfortunately, Erin's parents didn't believe that the entity was real and put her in therapy. She was relentlessly teased at school and called "ghost girl" for years. Luckily, she was quickly befriended by fellow Ghostbusters founding member Abby.

Founding Member: Abigail L. Yates, PhD

Dr. Abigail L. Yates (Abby for short) is another theoretical particle physicist. Straightforward, commanding, and honest to a fault, Abby has never been out for ghostbusting glory—her goal is to conduct groundbreaking research while protecting mankind from supernatural threats.

Abby has been Erin's friend and colleague for many years. The pair met in school and bonded easily over their fascination with the paranormal, which for Abby began at the tender age of four. Together they conducted highly advanced research at the high school level, presenting it at their school science fair as "The Durable but Not Impenetrable Barrier."

After completing her PhD, Abby held a research position at the Kenneth P. Higgins Science Institute for a number of years. It was there that she met another fellow Ghostbuster, Jillian Holtzmann.

Erin & Abby: Lifelong Friends

If the Ghostbusters have a heart, it is the friendship between founding members Abby and Erin. Their aforementioned research project, "The Durable but Not Impenetrable Barrier," helped them unravel Rowan the Destroyer's plot to unleash ghosts into our world.

Erin and Abby's research expanded through their college years, and they ultimately collaborated on a full-length book titled **Ghosts from Our Past: Both Literally and Figuratively: The Study of the Paranormal**.

When their book was released, the friends were invited to appear on a University of Michigan public television show. But having been taunted and teased as "ghost girl" for most of her life, Erin was worried about going public with her research. She wanted to be taken seriously as a scientist.

Erin failed to appear for the television show, causing a massive rift in her and Abby's friendship that lasted many years. It was only when Erin moved past her old insecurities that she was able to mend ties with Abby.

Today, with other founding members Holtzmann and Patty, the two stand strong as the cornerstone of our organization.

Founding Member: Jillian Holtzmann

Jillian Holtzmann (she prefers to be addressed as Holtzmann) is an engineer who, like Erin and Abby, specializes in theoretical particle physics. But where Abby and Erin focus on the research and hard science of ghost hunting, Holtzmann uses their research to create weapons and machines to combat and contain the paranormal.

Holtzmann met Abby shortly after a lab incident that lost her a job offer with a top nuclear research organization. She later joined Abby's lab at the Kenneth P. Higgins Science Institute.

It wasn't that bad... They said he moved a finger yesterday!

While some members of the community might find Holtzmann eccentric, she is a well-respected engineer and visionary.

With Holtzmann's technology, the Ghostbusters have advanced further than they ever thought possible. Her original weapons and traps paved the way for the (mostly) ghost-free world we know today.

Mastering the High Five

During their time at the Kenneth P. Higgins Science Institute, Abby and Holtzmann became inseparable and even came up with their own secret high five!

Bonding with your Ghostbusters team is extremely important and having your own code words, handshakes, and even high fives can go a long way in strengthening the partner bond.

DO NOT high-five Kevin. He makes these crazy shark-alligator arms. Very dangerous.

Use some of the tips below to create your own high five and share it with your fellow Ghostbusters.

- **The Wind-Up**: When winding up for a high five, keep your eye on your partner's elbow. This will ensure maximum hand-to-hand contact.
- **Don't Be Afraid to Blow It Up**: Adding a fist bump to a high-five combo is always a great touch, but "blowing it up" can take your fist bump to the next level. To incorporate this move, simply spread out your fingers after you bump fists and make a cool explosion sound.
- **Old School**: Did you cultivate awesome patty-cake skills when you were little? Put your skills to good use by clapping once and meeting your partner's hands, then repeat.
- **Around the World**: For this move slap your partner's hand high and then continue moving your arm down in an arc to slap their hand low.
- **Put It in Reverse**: Slap your partner's palm, then move your hand backward to slap the reverse side of their hand.

Founding Member: Patricia Tolan

Patricia Tolan (Patty for short) joined the Ghostbusters after working for New York City's public transportation system. It was here that she first encountered Rowan, whom she would later confront and help defeat as a Ghostbuster.

Raised with a fierce love of reading, Patty quickly became an indispensable member of the team for her extensive knowledge on a variety of topics, including the history of New York. Before she became a Ghostbuster, she was already able to identify the second ghost the Ghostbusters ever encountered, a Class IV semianchored entity whom the team called "Sparky." Patty's thorough knowledge and by-the-book style keeps the team on track.

Patty was instrumental in launching our organization. She secured the Ghostbusters' first vehicle, the Ecto-1, a hearse that was borrowed from her uncle, who owns a funeral home. She also created the Ghostbusters' iconic jumpsuits, which were made from repurposed subway uniforms.

Patty's Ghostbusters Book Club

One of the most important and time-consuming aspects of ghostbusting is sifting through research . . . though not necessarily the scientific kind. When investigating a Class III entity, determining the ghost's previous living identity can be key to beating it (see page 52).

To this end, Patty has formed a weekly book club that focuses on history and the paranormal. You can read up on the history of haunted buildings, share your thoughts on famous ghouls, and maybe even enjoy some of Kevin's homemade cookies.

Following the book discussion, Patty is available for help with online research. She has very high standards for her sources and for which paranormal groups can be trusted. (Hint: The *Ghost Jumpers* TV show is *not* on her list.)

But their theme song is so catchy!

We'll save a spot for you at our next meeting!

Kevin: The Ghostbusters' Loyal Receptionist

Kevin applied to be the Ghostbusters' receptionist after we acquired our first headquarters above a Chinese restaurant. Prior to Kevin, all the Ghostbusters had was an old answering machine—not exactly the best for paranormal emergencies.

Kevin lives at the Ghostbusters' headquarters, but that doesn't mean he's always on call. He doesn't work Wednesdays, and he doesn't answer the phone before ten a.m. Occasionally, he'll need to dash out for auditions, improv rehearsal, or saxophone lessons, so please be sure to answer the Ghostbusters' hotline if Kevin isn't at his post.

Kevin also dabbles in web design and even created a few logos for the Ghostbusters. ~~Unfortunately,~~ Luckily none were used as the final design.

A Brief History of Our Organization

The Beginning

Before the founding of Ghostbusters, Erin was still at Columbia University. It all began when Ed Mulgrave, a historian for the Aldridge Museum, visited Erin upon finding her and Abby's book, **Ghosts from Our Past: Both Literally and Figuratively: The Study of the Paranormal.** Ed wanted Erin's help in ridding the museum of a troublesome ghost.

Erin reluctantly teamed up with Abby and Holtzmann to investigate the ghost at the museum, and afterward, Abby posted a video from the investigation online. But when the video went viral, Erin was promptly fired from her post at Columbia.

Meanwhile, Abby and Holtzmann were eager to show Erin that the Kenneth P. Higgins Science Institute was much more open-minded about paranormal research than Columbia. But when they spoke with the dean about increasing their funding, he admitted that he'd forgotten their department still existed. He decided to pull their funding and close the paranormal research department for good.

The group went in search of a new home, somewhere they could "explore the unknown" and continue their research unimpeded.

Ghostbusters' First Headquarters

With nowhere to conduct their research, Erin, Abby, and Holtzmann quickly cleared out their lab at the Kenneth P. Higgins Science Institute and contacted a rental agent to help them look for a new headquarters. The agent initially showed them a few properties that were out of their price range, but they eventually landed in a space above Abby's favorite Chinese restaurant.

The space used to be a dining room for the restaurant below, so it was filled with chairs and tables and booths—not exactly ideal for a laboratory—but the Ghostbusters weren't discouraged! They used the tables to set up their equipment and research, and the booths acted as tiny conference rooms.

Plus, with Abby's favorite Chinese restaurant below them, they had plenty of brain food to help them work!

but NOT enough wontons!

The Ghostbusters' Logo

In the early days Kevin created several options for logos that the Ghostbusters considered, including a female cartoon ghost and a hot dog floating over a house.

Unfortunately, the group didn't feel that any of these options ~~were quite right for their new venture.~~ had anything to do with ghostbusting.

They needed an image that was serious but not sad, lighthearted but not ridiculous.

While working a case the group crossed paths with a graffiti artist who frequented the subway station where Patty worked. They asked him to describe a ghost he'd witnessed, and despite Patty's protests, he spray-painted a cartoon ghost on the subway wall.

Patty wanted the ghost removed, but instead, the artist painted a red circle with a line through it. Patty grabbed the artist's spray-paint can and chased him off, but Holtzmann thought the cartoon had potential, so she snapped a photo of it on her way out.

That cartoon became the Ghostbusters' official logo!

The Ghostbusters' Name

It may surprise you, but early on, the Ghostbusters went by another name. During our first investigations, we were known as the Conductors of the Metaphysical Examination. Being a bit long, the name was difficult for Kevin (and the public at large) to remember.

However, when word spread of Sparky the subway station ghost, video from the team's investigation aired on a local news station. A news reporter actually came up with our name while interviewing Martin Heiss, a famous paranormal debunker:

"A local team of paranormal investigators released a video of a proclaimed ghost . . . So, what do we think of these Ghostbusters?"

Erin fought against the name for a while—she felt it was too silly, too much like the ridiculous *Ghost Jumpers* TV series. Still, as much as Erin disliked the name, it stuck, and the Ghostbusters became just that—Ghostbusters.

Getting Down to Business: Ghostbusters Protocols, Procedures, and Precautions

Looking the Part: Uniforms

As mentioned, the Ghostbusters' uniforms were created by Patty. They were made from old subway uniforms and intended to protect the Ghostbusters from ectoplasm (see page 48).

For your own uniform, follow these simple rules:

- Uniforms must be worn at all times during an investigation where ghost contact is possible.

- Your standard issue Ghostbuster jumpsuit should be fastened up to your neck. It has reflective tape to ensure visibility in dark environments, and pockets for collecting evidence and storing additional equipment, such as a PKE meter (see page 44).

- Standard issue Ghostbuster boots should be worn at all times. Jumpsuit pants should be tucked into boots.

- Please refrain from rolling up sleeves, as contact with ectoplasm is possible. The long-term effects of exposure to ectoplasm are unknown at this time.* Be sure to wear your standard issue Ghostbuster gloves. (Note that your sleeves should not be tucked into your gloves). Yeah. That would look ridiculous.

- In addition to your uniform you will be given a proton pack. Proton packs are worn on the back and strapped around the waist. (See page 39 for further information on proton pack use and technology.)

---

*Several theories about ectoplasm exposure have been put forth by Abby and Erin, but further research is needed. Ghostbusters will be briefed when more information becomes available.

Getting Around:
Ghostbusters' Vehicles

What ghost-hunting case would be complete without a ride in the Ecto-1, the Ghostbusters' main company vehicle? Or the Ecto-2, our cool, mission-ready motorcycle?

Ecto-1

Patty procured this refurbished hearse from her uncle, who owns a funeral home. Holtzmann then modified and outfitted the hearse with the latest ghostbusting technology.

Its spacious interior has room for an entire team of Ghostbusters, as well as their gear and extra traps or weaponry.

Additional power packs and equipment are stored on the roof of the car. Please be sure these are safely secured before you exit the garage.

RESPECT
THE SIREN
PLEASE

On official missions Ghostbusters are encouraged to use the lights and siren sparingly, and only in true paranormal emergencies. If it's necessary to clear the street, the Ecto-1 also has a loudspeaker that can be activated from inside the vehicle.

Ecto-2

For smaller-scale missions Ghostbusters are welcome to take the Ecto-2, an old motorcycle outfitted for use by Kevin. Storage on the Ecto-2 is limited, so bear this in mind when considering the best vehicle for your needs.

Laboratory Safety and Precautions

Of course, being a Ghostbuster isn't just about being in the field. There is a great deal of research involved as well, so be prepared for many late nights in the lab.

As founding member Holtzmann loves to say, "To be clear, nothing in this lab is safe," and it's important that you bear this in mind when entering the laboratory.

WARNING
PARTS MAY FALL OFF

Below are some other
important rules to follow:

- Much of the equipment you'll see in the lab from day to day is in development or repair. As such, it could be unstable and should not be touched unless Holtzmann has given you express permission to do so.

- Holtzmann may ask you to participate in an experiment. In this case, please ~~follow her instructions carefully~~ *run away quickly* to ensure your safety.

- Proper lab attire should be worn at all times: goggles, gloves, closed-toe shoes, and pants. If you have long hair, be sure to tie it back.

- Fire extinguishers are located on the north and south walls of the lab. Since Holtzmann often listens to music while working, make sure to extinguish any fires you might see in the lab immediately, as she might not have noticed them.

Evolution of
the Proton Pack

Proton Box

Developed by
Holtzmann after the
Ghostbusters left the
Kenneth P. Higgins
Science Institute.
The box was still
in development

the first time it was used during the Ghostbusters'
encounter with Sparky, the aforementioned
Class IV entity in the Seward Street subway station.
The machine was also quite large and cumbersome
and had to be carted to the station.

The box had the earliest known version of the
proton wand. The proton wand shoots a proton
stream, which freezes ghosts in place. Because
the proton box wasn't finished, it emitted a weak
proton stream that only managed to work on ghosts
in close proximity (roughly two feet from the box).

The proton box was destroyed during its first
field test—crushed by a subway car.

Proton Packs

Based on the findings from the Ghostbusters' field test with the proton box, Holtzmann made several modifications. She first shrank the original

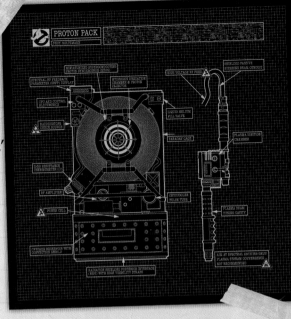

machinery, making the new proton pack portable and safe to wear. Carrying the system as a backpack also allowed the wearer maximum flexibility during a paranormal encounter.

Holtzmann then boosted the proton stream's power and increased the range of the proton wand by using microfabricated dielectric laser accelerators to speed up the particles before they enter the DLA device.

In short, the Ghostbusters could now freeze ghosts in place from farther away!

This isn't on the test, right??

Ghost Trap

Prior to their exit from the Kenneth P. Higgins Science Institute, Abby and Holtzmann had a breakthrough on a hollow laser that completed the reverse tractor beam Erin and Abby had written about together in their first book. With this development, the Ghostbusters would at last be able to design a trap that could suck ghosts inside once they were within range.

The trap itself contains spectrally reflective plating and shielded containment doors, which prevent ghosts from escaping once inside. An occupancy indicator near the trap's handle signals if you've caught a ghost. The light turns from red to green when a ghost is inside.

IMPORTANT: The trap should only be carried by the handle, since parts of it are radioactive.

Translation: no kissing the trap, Erin.

Additional Weaponry

Following the first successful test run of the ghost trap, Holtzmann refined the proton packs' accuracy and power. She then created a few special goodies for use in fighting multiple ghosts at once.

The first were proton grenades, which Patty favors. These release a proton blast that can eliminate multiple ghosts at once—perfect if you ever find yourself surrounded by a ghostly siege.

Holtzmann also developed a set of smaller proton guns. Rather than freeze ghosts, these small guns can destroy an apparition quickly. Great for use on smaller, weaker entities.

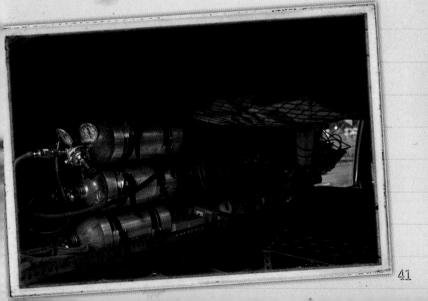

- Crossing Streams -

When on a group mission, it may become necessary to use multiple proton streams to take down an entity. This would happen if your target has too much energy to be trapped with a single stream. In this case you will need to combine streams with your fellow Ghostbusters to take down the apparition.

Should this become necessary, take caution. Accidentally crossing streams can cause a counterreaction; the beam will shoot back at you, causing every atom in your body to simultaneously explode.

BOOM!

The ONLY circumstance in which you should intentionally cross streams is in closing a ghost portal. Ghost portals emit energy, so bouncing energy back into the portal is the only way to close it. If you require extra energy, we recommend using a high-concentration electron blast to finish the job. Extra negative-charge containment canisters can be found on top of the Ecto-1.

Other Ghostbusting Tools

Walkie-Talkies

Standard issue walkie-talkies should be taken on all missions and are necessary to ensure effective communication between teammates.

PKE Meter

PKE stands for "psychokinetic energy." A PKE meter detects ghostly energy and can direct you to areas in which such energy is concentrated. When a ghost is near, the antennae on the PKE meter spins and will speed up the closer you get. Remember to approach your entity cautiously, as it could be malevolent.

Note: The PKE meter is fairly small and can be stored in one of the larger pockets on your jumpsuit.

Recording Devices

When in the field always bring multiple video and audio recording devices. Why so many? If you hear an abnormal, possibly otherworldly sound, you can use the recordings to triangulate the source.

Even if a ghost isn't found, you'll be able to rule out other causes of the noise. These practices keep our organization scientifically sound and help us sort the fake hauntings from the real ones.

Terminology

Signs of the Paranormal

In determining whether a haunting is real or a hoax, just remember PEACE:

- **P**KE: Be sure to keep your PKE meter out and at the ready; a spike in the energy reading may mean an entity is close.
- **E**ctoplasm: This gelatinous residue on walls, ceilings, and floors is a good indicator of an apparition. (See page 48 for more information.)
- **A**P-xH Shift: You can tell if a shift has occurred if your ears pop.
- **C**old air: A drop in temperature usually indicates that a spirit is near; this is because an entity will draw energy from the air around it, leaving a space cold.
- **E**VP: Be sure to review your recording devices once you're back at headquarters. EVP, or electronic voice phenomenon, may show up on your recordings. These sounds can be interpreted as messages from beyond our world.

Ectoplasm

Perhaps the most important sign of an otherworldly presence is ectoplasm. Ectoplasm is a slimy, clear-to-greenish substance that paranormal entities tend to spew or project when they interact with something from our plane of existence.

Ectoplasm is incredibly common in the ghost-hunting business, and you can expect to encounter it frequently. Though the substance produces no short-term harm to humans, most Ghostbusters prefer to have as little contact with ectoplasm as possible. Please note that the long-term effects of exposure to ectoplasm (if any) have yet not been tested.

ECTO

HAZARD

Ectoplasm has also been referred to as "ghost slime," leading to the slang term "slimed," a verb that means "to be spewed with ectoplasm." The technical term for "slimed" is "ectoprojected," and this is the term you should use in your reports.

The Seven Classes of Ghosts

The first step in conducting a paranormal investigation is to identify your entity as quickly as possible. Abby and Erin have pulled together their research to create the ghost classification system in the following pages, and it has proven invaluable to our success.

Class I

These undeveloped forms are commonly referred to as "vapors" since they are difficult to see and take no definite shape. (Though note that "vapor" can be used to describe other classes as well.) They might appear as spectral lights, disembodied voices or sounds, ectoplasmic mists, etc. They are unable to interact with physical objects.

Class II

Class II ghosts typically take a form that is incomplete, such as a ghostly hand or limbless torso. Ghosts in this class and up can manipulate physical objects (meaning they can throw, push, grab, and so on), so be sure to use caution when engaging.

Class III

Apparitions are assigned to this category when a distinct human form is evident, but the identity of the ghost is unknown. Class III ghosts are considered one of the trickier classes to deal with, as they are able to defend themselves well against attacks.

Class IV

When the identity of a Class III ghost is established, it is reassigned to Class IV. This usually makes the ghost easier to deal with, as research can be done into the ghost's former life. Attempts to communicate with the entity have proven successful in some cases.

Class V

Class V ghosts are ectoplasmic manifestations of definite but nonhuman form. Erin and Abby have theorized that Class V entities are born from emotionally charged events, which would explain the sometimes terrifying forms they take. Ghosts of this class can be difficult to take down and usually require a team.

Class VI

This class is reserved for ghosts of nonhuman life-forms, such as animals. In the moments leading up to the battle against Rowan the Destroyer, a spectral polar bear from this class was seen wandering around Park Avenue. As we've seen with Class V, nonhuman ghosts can be incredibly difficult to deal with, but research into habitats and natural enemies can aid in eliminating these spirits.

Class VII

By far the most dangerous class of entities, these powerful, malevolent beings are generally referred to as "metaspecters" or, more commonly, "demons." These apparitions not only possess fierce strength but also have the ability to command other forms, both living and otherworldly. Neutralizing such forces is incredibly difficult, as these beings fall outside the scope of usual Ghostbusting procedures. When possible, it is simply best to prevent these spirits from entering the physical realm at all.

Rating Ghostly Interactions

As you conduct your Ghostbusters investigations, it is extremely important to canvass the scene of the haunting and interview witnesses. If no witnesses are available, you can always speak with so-called "secondary witnesses"—neighbors, utility workers, and people who may have interacted indirectly with the scene.

In these interviews we find that it helps to have a basis upon which to rate a ghostly interaction and have compiled one, below:

- **T1**: Witnesses report seeing an apparition but made no contact.

- **T2**: Entity has interacted with humans. Beginning at this level, traces of ectoplasm can be found at the site of the haunting.

- **T3**: The apparition was able to, through whatever means, inspire intense fear in a human. Witnesses may report excessive nightmares and paranoia following a T3 interaction.

- **T4**: The ghost means harm to humans and may have tried throwing an object, starting a fire, causing a person to trip, etc.

- **T5**: The entity is malevolent and has harmed and/ or possessed a human. Ghosts who have committed T5 interactions are intensely powerful and should be dealt with carefully.

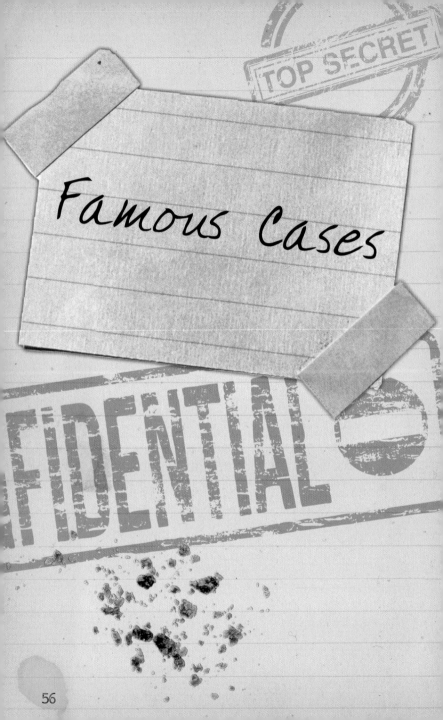

Famous Cases

The Durable but Not Impenetrable Barrier!

At Ghostbusters we have one main mission:
Protect the barrier.

But what exactly is the barrier?

As teenaged researchers of the paranormal, Erin and Abby presented a science fair project called "The Durable but Not Impenetrable Barrier." It contained an epic score of ghostly research performed as a rap:

"The barrier stops ghosts from coming through. It is the only line of defense in the portal betwixt the worlds of the living and the dead."

While the barrier is able to protect our world from the majority of paranormal threats, some entities do break through, and when they do, it's up to us to stop them.

At the beginning of this guide, we told you that a book can become a terrible weapon, and Erin and Abby know that better than anyone. Rowan the Destroyer, one of the Ghostbusters' most fearsome enemies, read Abby and Erin's book, **Ghosts from Our Past**. He used their research to create a machine that could tear a hole in the barrier between our world and the ghost world, unleashing the paranormal on mankind.

Erin discovered a copy of their book in Rowan's lair beneath the Mercado Hotel and brought it back to her apartment. Flipping through the pages, Erin saw that Rowan had scribbled notes in the margins—notes like attracting the paranormal and the first cataclysm.

But what was even more terrifying was a doodle Rowan had done on the blank pages at the back of the book: a sketch of New York City being ripped apart by ghosts. In the center was a massive being with Rowan's face. Beside the sketch was a note:

THE FOURTH
CATACLYSM—
I WILL LEAD THEM.

But just how did Rowan use Erin and Abby's book to such evil ends?

– Ley Lines –

Rowan began his work by studying the ley lines in New York City. Ley lines are a hidden network of energy lines across the Earth—currents of supernatural energy. From Erin's field notes:

"Supposedly, if you look at sacred sites and weird events around the world, you can draw a line between them. And where the lines intersect creates an unusually powerful spot."

▲DANGER
THE MAGNET IS
ALWAYS ON

For years Erin had dismissed ley lines as implausible. The lines seemed too likely to happen at random; after all, what qualifies as a sacred site or a strange event?

But when ghost sightings in New York exploded, Erin began plotting the sightings on a map and drawing lines between them. These lines overlapped perfectly with an existing map of ley lines in the city. That's when the team worked out that Rowan was charging up the ley lines in order to break the ghost barrier. Let's take a closer look at some of the ghosts who made it through.

Rowan's Devices

To charge the ley lines, Rowan needed to attract spirits to several precise locations. It was important that the ghosts appear right along the ley lines so that they could be properly charged. The first four cases the Ghostbusters investigated were all caused by Rowan as part of his master plan.

Patty was the first to actually meet Rowan. Prior to joining the Ghostbusters, Patty encountered him at the Seward Street subway station where she worked. Rowan planted a small humming, sparking device near the

subway tracks. The device quickly burned up, and the Ghostbusters found remnants of it.

The team wasn't entirely sure what the contraption was until they encountered a second, working machine at the Stonebrook Theatre. It turned out to be a hyper-ionization device, which supercharges ghosts, making them strong enough to penetrate the barrier.

The Historic Aldridge Mansion

Historic Aldridge Mansion is the only nineteenth-century home in New York City preserved both inside and out. The sprawling manor has been meticulously maintained exactly as its former owner, the wealthy Sir Aldridge, left it.

The mansion features an incredible two-floor library with all its original volumes intact as well as beautiful artwork of the Aldridge family. Visitors can see meticulously crafted evening gowns and suits on display, taken right from the wardrobes of the Aldridges.

Afternoon tea is available daily in the parlor, where Sir and Lady Aldridge entertained their many wealthy guests, among whom were some of the brightest artists and writers of their generation.

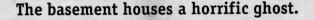

The basement houses a horrific ghost.

Gertrude
Class IV Apparition

Gertrude Aldridge, the eldest daughter of Sir Aldridge, was the first ghost ever encountered by the fledgling Ghostbusters.

The story goes that one horrible night, Gertrude murdered all the Aldridge servants in their sleep. Her family should have turned Gertrude over to the police, but instead, her father locked her in the basement. Years later, the new owner had the basement door sealed shut, having repeatedly heard strange sounds coming from down there. Was the ghost of Gertrude haunting the basement?

For many years tour guides at the mansion told this story to frighten visitors, but the story, it turns out, was true. Gertrude had been haunting the mansion as a Class IV apparition with all the classic signs—AP-xH shift, ectoplasmic residue, and high PKE readings.

Erin attempted to make friendly contact with the spirit, but the apparition ectoprojected onto her.

SLIMED

Seward Street Subway Station

As you now know, before Patty joined the Ghostbusters, she worked for the New York City subway at a booth in the Seward Street station. With her extensive knowledge of the city's history, Patty knew that the station had been built right below the old York prison, the first prison in New York to execute prisoners by electric chair. She said she always had a feeling that something strange was going on there.

Patty contacted the Ghostbusters because of a ghost encounter she had in the station.

Sparky
Class IV Semianchored Entity

Little is known about Sparky, the Class IV entity who the Ghostbusters encountered in the Seward Street station. He appeared as a tall, thin, pale man with yellow eyes, wearing a dated prison uniform.

We've already been over the fact that one of Rowan's machines was found at the scene of the investigation; this explained why Sparky was even more ionized than Gertrude, the previous ghost they'd encountered. Sparky's increased power was almost too much for Holtzmann's early proton box to handle.

Backstage at the
Stonebrook Theatre

The Stonebrook Theatre hosts a variety of concerts each year, including the local battle of the bands. A network of hallways under the theatre connects people to dressing rooms, costume closets, and other storage spaces.

Jonathan, the manager, insisted that he'd never experienced anything strange at the theatre, but after Rowan placed one of his devices there, things took a turn for the worse. That very night an entity rushed out of a wall vent and attacked the custodian, Fernando. "No one should ever have to encounter that kind of evil," Jonathan said before wishing the Ghostbusters luck in catching it.

Mayhem
Class III Vapor

The Ghostbusters met with the Class III vapor they named "Mayhem" during their sweep of the Stonebrook Theatre. The entity possessed a mannequin from one of the storage rooms and used it to attack Patty. While terrifying, the encounter proved Abby's long-held theories about full paratransferral embodiment.

Once they destroyed the mannequin with proton blasts, the ghost proceeded to attack a band performing onstage. It took four proton beams to bring the entity down and trap it in Holtzmann's newly made ghost trap.

Unfortunately, the ghost was released by Erin shortly thereafter and is still at large.

THANKS, ERIN.

Rowan

During his life, Rowan was a gifted physicist with advanced degrees from Stanford and MIT. It is unknown what caused him to use his talents for evil, but it's clear that he bears great resentment toward other humans.

Rowan took a job as a custodian for the Mercado Hotel, a historic inn at the heart of New York City that also stands at the intersection of several powerful ley lines. As Patty will tell you, the lines have caused many strange occurrences dating back to the 1600s, before the city was even established.

Using his extensive knowledge of high-energy density physics, Rowan created the aforementioned devices to charge the ley lines. Beneath the Mercado, he built a master device that could harness the energy generated to break the barrier between the world of the living and the dead.

Rowan the Destroyer

Class VII Metaspecter

Just as Rowan finished charging his device, the
Ghostbusters used a map of ley lines to figure out
the location of Rowan's lair. But when they cornered
Rowan there, he became a ghost. At first the
Ghostbusters were confused by this turn of events,
until Erin figured out that it was all part of Rowan's
plan: To lead the ghosts, he had to become a ghost
himself.

Now free of his body, Rowan was able to activate
his machine and break the barrier. Ghosts poured
out of the Mercado Hotel, and despite attempts from
the military and police to contain the threat, Rowan
was succeeding in destroying the city.

As a ghost, Rowan possessed powers only
exhibited by a Class VII metaspecter. He was able to
control police and military officers, forcing them to
dance and then freezing them in place. Rowan also
possessed two people (Abby and Kevin), and, in his
ghost form, was able to manipulate his appearance.

In the end Rowan was too strong to be defeated.
The Ghostbusters managed to reverse the flow of the
ghost portal, sucking him back into the ghost world
before they sealed off the barrier once again.

Slimer
Class V

A Class V
full-roaming vapor,
Slimer is a rather
grotesque entity made
of ectoplasm (thus the
name Slimer). During
the battle against Rowan the Destroyer, Slimer stole
the Ecto-1 and took it for a joyride around the city,
picking up other ghosts (including an apparently
female Slimette) as he went.

The Ghostbusters tricked him into driving the
Ecto-1 into the ghost portal. The car was loaded with
extra negative-charge containment canisters, and the
power boost was what prompted the portal to close,
with Slimer, luckily, on the other side.

Stay-Puft Marshmallow Man Class VI

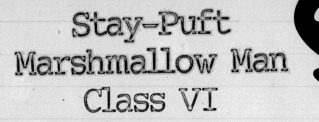

Another ghost group encountered during the battle was a creepy 1920s parade. The parade served as a distraction for many ghosts, which prevented more extensive damage to the city. The parade balloons themselves, as it turned out, were actually ghosts, and when they caught sight of the Ghostbusters, they attacked.

One of the balloons was a Class VI possession in the shape of the Stay-Puft Marshmallow Man with (obvious) temporal displacement.

In other words, the ghost belonged to a different time period.

The Ghostbusters tried to attack it with their proton packs but were crushed into the ground. Fortunately, Erin arrived and was able to pop the balloon and remove the entity.

Ghost Possession

Spectral (or ghost) possession describes any time a ghost takes control of something from our world. This could be a person, an animal, or even an object.

Spectral possession is always something to look out for in the field. Even the best of us, like Abby and Kevin, have been victims of possession. If you fear that you or one of your teammates has been compromised, be sure to check for ectoplasmic discharge from the nose, ears, or mouth.

Ejecting a spirit from a possessed object is fairly straightforward—a proton blast should do the trick.

Be sure that your teammates are standing by to trap the ghost once it is expelled.

DO NOT use this same strategy on a possessed person or animal, however. Instead, corner the possessed person. If the ghost does not flee immediately, try jolting the person or, in more severe cases, administering a slap to the face. The spirit will usually free its victim when it sees no other means of escape.

Codes of Conduct and Perks

Keeping a Low Profile

As a Ghostbuster it's important to not attract the attention of the public. We frequently team up with a variety of local, state, and federal government agencies in defending the public, and they would prefer we keep our work quiet.

This is why we ask that Ghostbusters use the lights and siren on the Ecto-1 sparingly and why we ask you to keep this handbook closely guarded. Many people aren't prepared to believe in the paranormal—they can't wrap their minds around it. And besides, the threats we deal with are fairly scary to the general public; the average citizen doesn't need to know about every danger facing him or her.

So we drive a hearse with an unauthorized siren.

CAUTION
STAY BACK
OVER 500 FT
NOT RESPONSIBLE
FOR DAMAGE

The Problem with Going Public

Having read the previous pages, you might be wondering if the Ghostbusters receive any kind of recognition for our hard work. By and large, the answer is no. Much of the general public believes that we are frauds, but comfort yourself in knowing that should these people find themselves faced with a paranormal problem, we are the ones they'll turn to.

For quite some time this lack of recognition bothered Erin. She liked the respect that came with being a more mainstream scientist and hated that her name was dragged through the mud when she became a Ghostbuster. But luckily, Abby had some wise words for her:

"You think it's been easy, devoting my life to all this? I've been called 'weird' every day of my life since I was four years old, and I hate it. But I focus on what matters. We discovered all sorts of new things. I get to work with my friends. I feel pretty lucky."

Erin took these words to heart and hasn't looked back since. In many ways being a Ghostbuster and doing what we do is its own reward. That having been said, there are still some perks to the job.

Pranks

Though we acknowledge that ghosts and fun usually go hand in hand, Erin has asked that pranking be kept to a minimum and that it not involve any deadly consequences.

Examples of unacceptable pranks include:

- Farting into a recording device and attempting to pass it off as an EVP reading (electronic voice phenomenon—ghost speech).

- Camouflaging yourself in order to scare your partner while in the field.

- Repeatedly driving just out of reach to prevent a teammate from getting into the Ecto-1 while on a mission.

New recruits are reminded that assisting in performing a prank will result in the same punishment as executing a prank.

GHOST DID IT

Complimentary Meals

If you find yourself working through lunch or staying late to finish a project, feel free to dial 555-0128 and order a meal on us. This is the number for the Chinese restaurant we used to work above.

Not enough wontons!

Once, Abby had a
fierce, ongoing battle
with the restaurant
and their delivery
guy, Benny.
Abby could never
get more than
one wonton in
her soup—hardly
the most filling
meal. And even
though we were
housed right above the
restaurant, it still took Benny sometimes over an hour
to deliver her food.

But after the Ghostbusters saved New York, Benny
was so grateful that he convinced the restaurant to
pack her soup full of wontons. To this day we receive
a discount at the restaurant and expedited free
delivery, so order whatever you'd like!

A Glimpse into the Unknown

Erin and Abby released another book that chronicled their field research leading up to, and during the battle against, Rowan the Destroyer:

A Glimpse into the Unknown: A Journey into a Portal; Catching Sight of the Other Dimension: Discovering the Undiscoverable: A Curiosity Piqued and Peaked

Of course, the most fascinating chapters are perhaps those about what happened when Abby and Erin fell through the ghost portal shortly before Slimer drove the Ecto-1 through. To the surprise of Patty and Holtzmann, the two scientists returned with white hair. . . .

But we'd hate to spoil it for you! Be sure to see Kevin about picking up a copy of the book from the Ghostbusters' library.

Ghostbusters Today

Today the Ghostbusters stand as a silent reminder to all ghosts, specters, and apparitions that mankind is defended.

Following our triumph over Rowan the Destroyer, the mayor's office purchased the Ghostbusters a more permanent home in a beautiful loft, converted from an old firehouse. They encouraged us to continue conducting and sharing our research to help the government defend the city from the paranormal.

There are citizens who appreciate the Ghostbusters and believe in what we do, but there are others who continue to mock our cause. It's best to keep any negative thoughts and doubt from your mind—entities can feed off negative energy, and you risk putting your teammates in danger.

Final Test

Now that you've read up on our history and procedures, it's time to test your knowledge and see what you've learned! Once you pass this test, feel free to turn the page for your honorary Ghostbusters certificate.

1.   A witness reports a haunting; they experienced an entity that severed a chandelier cord, nearly causing the witness to be crushed. How would you rate this interaction?

a. Cool!   b. T1   c. T4

2.   You encounter an apparition with a distinct human form but are unable to determine its identity. What class does this spirit belong to?

a. Class III   b. Class VI   c. Class IV

3.   How would you dispense with a spectrally possessed car?

a. attempt contact   b. proton blast   c. get a mechanic

4.   What is the official term for "slimed"?

a. ectoprojected   b. ectospewed   c. grossed out

5. What acronym do we use when looking for signs of the paranormal in the field?

a. WAR   **b.** MECHS   **c.** PEACE

6. What should be your main consideration in taking the Ecto-2 on a mission rather than the Ecto-1?

a. speed   **b.** storage space   **c.** cool factor

7. Which of the following is not a useful tool for Ghostbusters missions?

a. walkie-talkie   **b.** PKE meter   **c.** bunny slippers

8. In researching an apparition, which of the following is *not* a reliable source, according to Patty?

a. *Ghost Jumpers*   **b.** *Ghosts from Our Past*   **c.** newspapers

9. Prior to founding the Ghostbusters, Erin was up for tenure at which university?

a. Columbia University   **b.** Stanford University   **c.** MIT

10. When in the lab, do not touch anything unless . . .

a. it's buzzing   **b.** Holzmann tells you to   **c.** it's shiny

ANSWERS: 1. c   2. a   3. b   4. a   5. c   6. b   7. c   8. a   9. a   10. b

Certificate

Congratulations!

The Ghostbusters declare
that today you are an
honorary Ghostbuster!

You have read the protocols,
checked the case files, and done
the research necessary to
earn you a privileged spot
among our ranks.

You've come to the end of this guide, but that doesn't mean your journey is over. A new supernatural world awaits you in our venerable organization. Before you know it, you'll be seizing specters with the best of them, and we can't wait to see you for your first day of Ghostbusters casework! In the meantime be sure to guard this book and study it well—the fate of our world depends on you.